# Radha Dances

*To Piya-Vivaan, who bring out the storyteller in me – A.K.R.*

*To the children who have lost their hearing because of war – R.S.*

First published in India by HarperCollins Children's Books 2026
An imprint of HarperCollins Publishers
HarperCollins Publishers India, Cyber City,
Building 10-A, Gurugram, Haryana-122002, India
www.harpercollins.co.in

2 4 6 8 10 9 7 5 3 1



P-ISBN: 978-93-6989-679-0
E-ISBN: 978-93-6989-335-5

Typeset in 13/17 Arima Koshi
by HarperCollins *Publishers* India Pvt. Ltd

Printed and bound at Nutech Print Services Pvt. Ltd.

This book is printed on FSC® certified paper
which ensures responsible forest management.

HarperCollins Publishers, Macken House, 39/40 Mayor Street Upper, Dublin 1,
D01 C9W8, Ireland

*

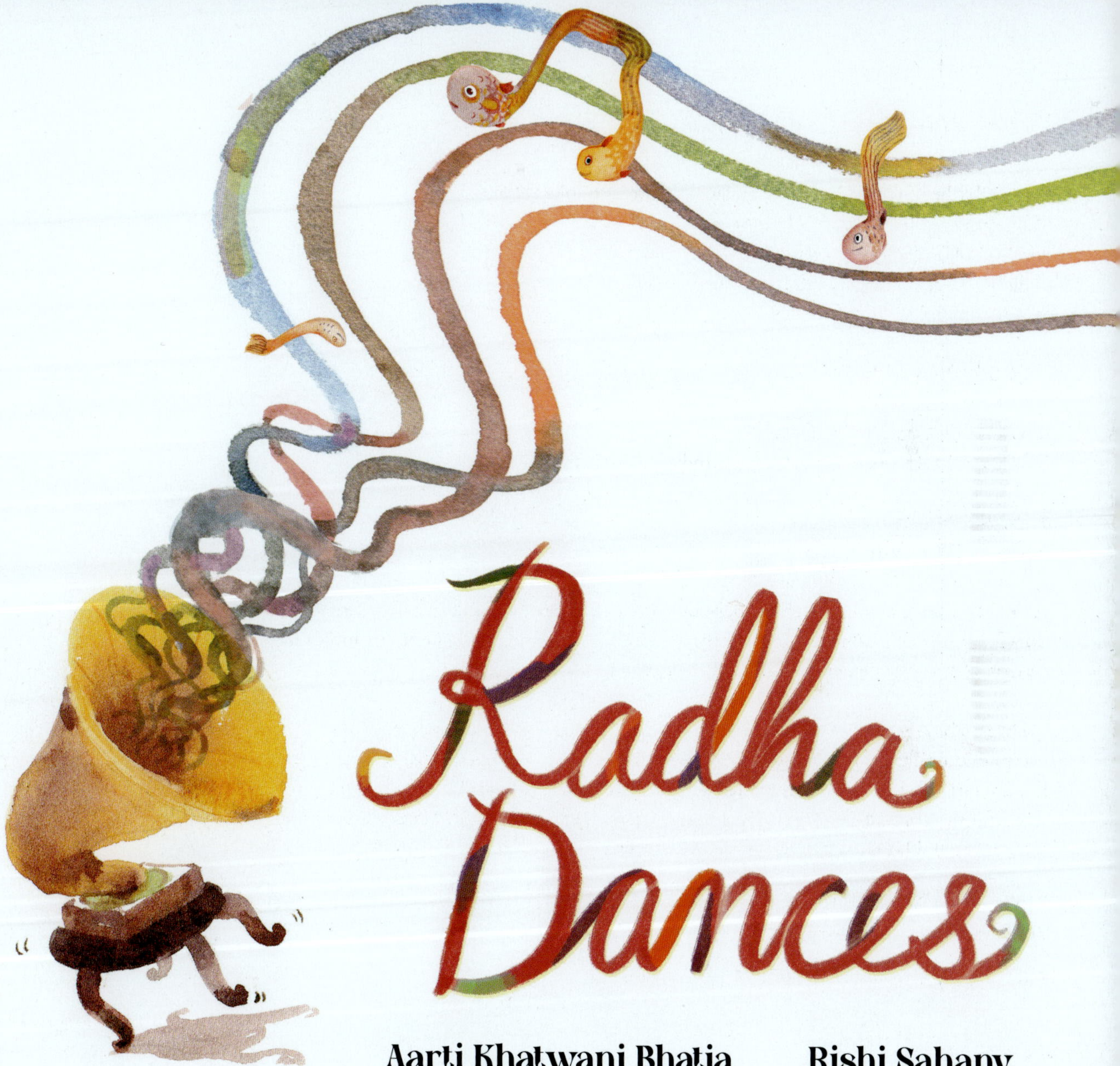

# Radha Dances

Aarti Khatwani Bhatia      Rishi Sahany

HC CB
HARPERCOLLINS
CHILDREN'S BOOKS

The rooster did not go
'kukdukooo'.

The vehicles did not go
'honk, honk, beeeeep'.

The kettle did not go ‘wheeeeeee’.

The newspaper boy’s cycle did not go ‘tring-tring’.

Maa and Paa sipped their
tea in the warm sunlight.
Radha sat with them,
watching this quiet world.

The warmth of the sun's first ray
woke her up.

The taste of dust in her mouth told
her that the world had started
moving outside.

The aroma from the kitli said
the tea was ready.

The newspaper's flight showed her that the paper boy was making his rounds.

But one thing made her happier than hot tea and cold mornings.

The dance class across the street.

Arms moved like waves,
Feet tapped together,
Graceful movements in colourful clothes.

As the teacher clapped,
and the kids danced...

so did Radha.

One day, the teacher saw Radha dancing. She immediately hid.

After that day, Radha did not go to the balcony.

A few days later, there was a familiar face at Radha's doorstep. The teacher had come to meet the little girl who danced to her snaps and claps from across the street. She wanted Radha to join her class.

Radha saw the exact moment the teacher came to know—

Radha couldn't hear.

Radha hid again. The teacher extended her hand.
Radha stayed behind the curtain.

The teacher clapped.
Radha stepped out.

The teacher snapped.
Radha tapped a foot.

The teacher started snapping and clapping. Radha moved her body in tune.

Her parents looked on in awe.

Radha enrolled in the dance class but it was nothing like dancing in her balcony.

At times, Radha would
go out of rhythm,
miss a step,
bump into other kids
or fall down.

How would she ever learn
to dance like the others?

Heartbroken, Radha went back to standing in her balcony, watching the other kids from afar.

Then, one day, a strong breeze swept through her hair. Radha looked up.

The curtain was moving freely, as if dancing on its own. A smile grew on Radha's face. Perhaps, she did not need a class.

Perhaps, she was meant to dance differently.

And so Radha began a new class.

'Clink-clank, clink-clink'
Maa banged the
plate with a stick.

'Ta-taa-ta-ta-taa',
danced Radha.

‘Thud-thud, thump-thump’
went the floor around Paa’s
old music-box.

‘Hop-hop, twist-and-twirl’
danced Radha.

Every once in a while
the teacher came to help.

Slowly, Radha began to find music in everything.

In the swaying breeze and the flowing water,

In the flickering lightning and the thundering rain—

Radha learnt to dance to the world.

Now, when she stepped
out in her balcony,

Arms painted waves in the air.
Feet tapped to everything she felt.

Gracefully moving
in colourful clothes,

Radha danced to no music.

**Aarti Khatwani Bhatia** has an MBA from NMIMS, Mumbai. After years of working with multinational companies like ConAgra Foods and Red Bull, she finally found her calling in stories. She has written for brands like Aveeno Baby, Nestle, Dabur, Preganews, Luvlap, Pediasure, Dove, Casio, and many more.

Her short story *You Come First* won the Silver Story of the Year in the international short-story writing competition at IFP 2022. When not sleeping, she is either telling her kids a story, or creating one with them. And when sleeping, well then she is just sleeping for she loves doing that as much as she loves telling stories!

**Rishi Sahany** is an animation filmmaker, painter and illustrator. He loves to draw stories, swim in open waters, observe fishes under water, spy on water-hen drying under the sun and also likes accompanying snakes when they are crossing the river.

He won the prestigious National Award 2015 as an Animation Director, for the film 'Sound of Joy'. He also wrote and directed an animated short film *Poly-ticks*, a political satire.

For the last five years, he has been writing and illustrating for children's literature. *Bhalu ka nakhoon* and *SaReGaMaPakshi* have both been recognised by children's literature awards in the year 2024-25. Rishi loves to travel alone and idling away time in a quaint village is the only goal on his itinerary.